For the Mountain Laurel Waldorf School—
you will always be home

GS

For my mum

MG

 • First US edition 2021 • Library of Congress Catalog Card Number pending • ISBN 978-1-5362-1115-3 • This book was typeset in Futura. The illustrations were done in watercolor, gouache, and colored pencil. Candlewick Press, 99 Dover Street, Somerville, Massachusetts 02144 • www.candlewick.com
Printed in Shenzhen, Guangdong, China • 20 21 22 23 24 25 CCP 10 9 8 7 6 5 4 3 2 1

[M]IDNIGHT FAIR

Gideon Sterer illustrated by Mariachiara Di Giorgio

CANDLEWICK PRESS

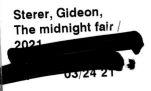

COUNTY FAIR

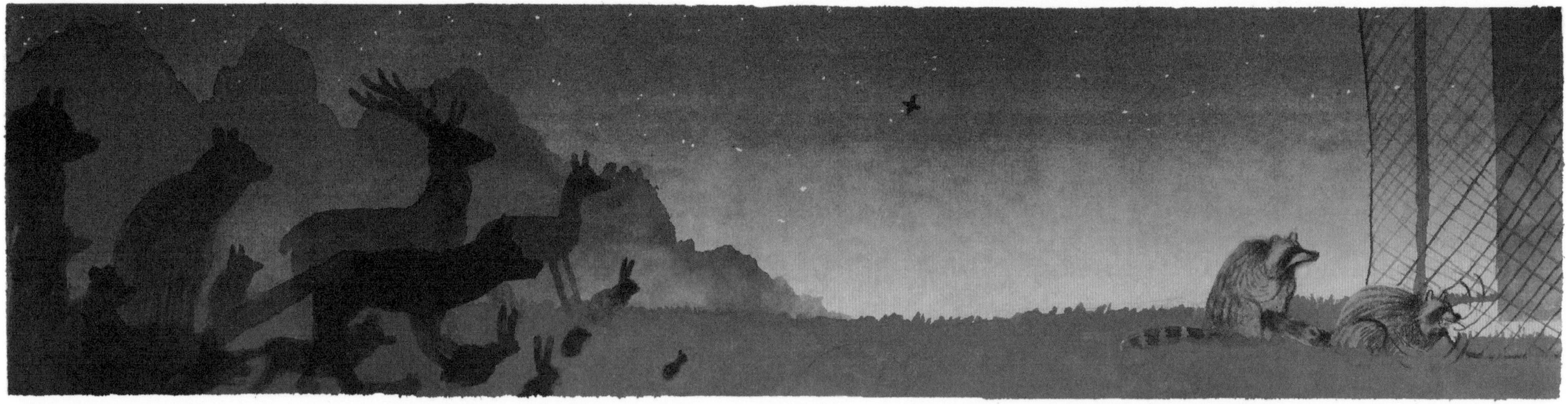

ROTOR
ICKETS

CYCLO
CANDY
COLD DRINKS

POPCORN
COTTON CANDY
POP POP

HOOK
A
Swa

Dante's Infer
PIZZA
PALM RE
DANTE'S INFERNO
HOT DOG
EXTRAS
FRENCH F
LARGE
$4.00
SMALL
$2.00
Veggie Dogs
DIET

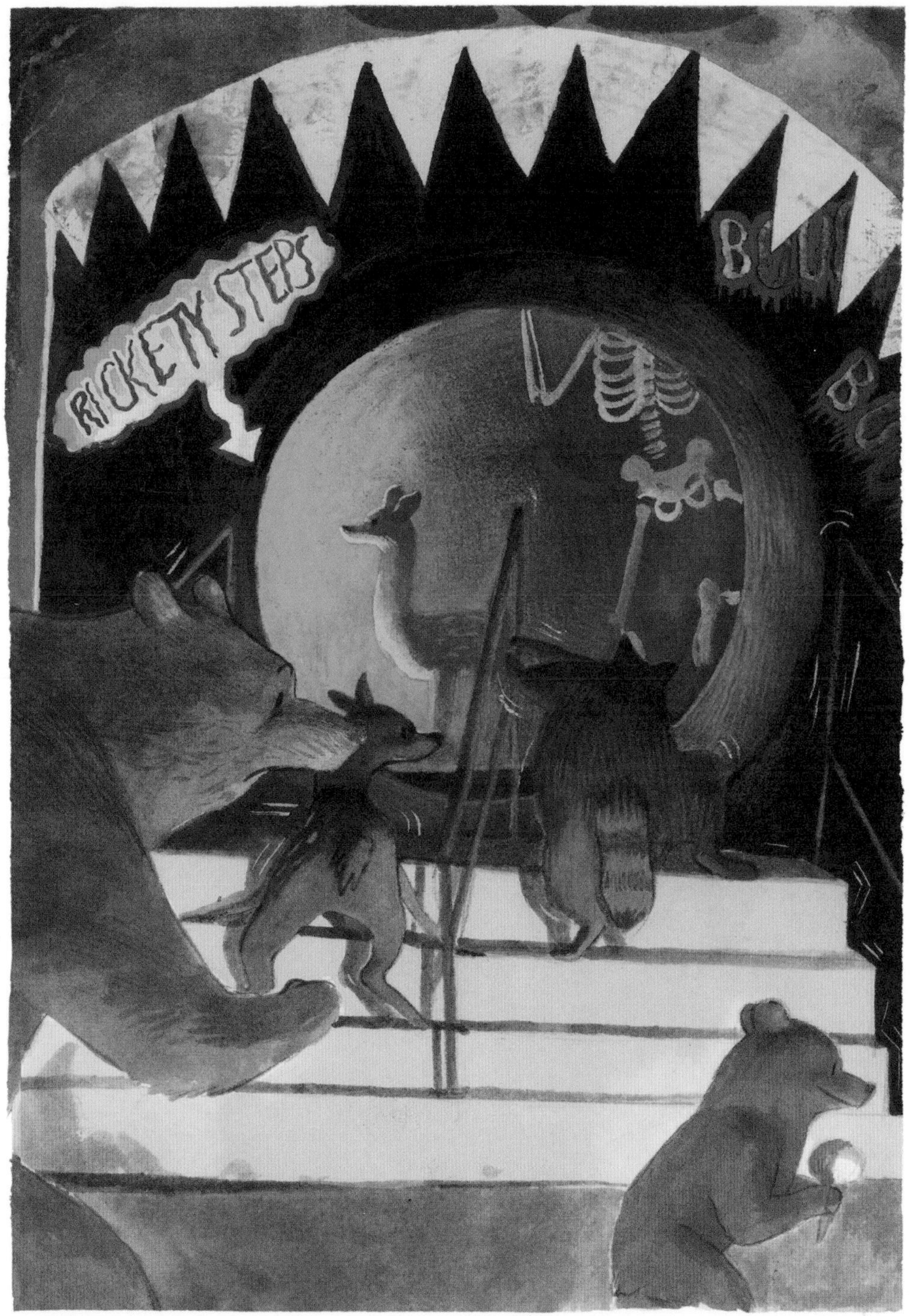
RICKETY STEPS

TICKETS

Soft

POP
Tickets

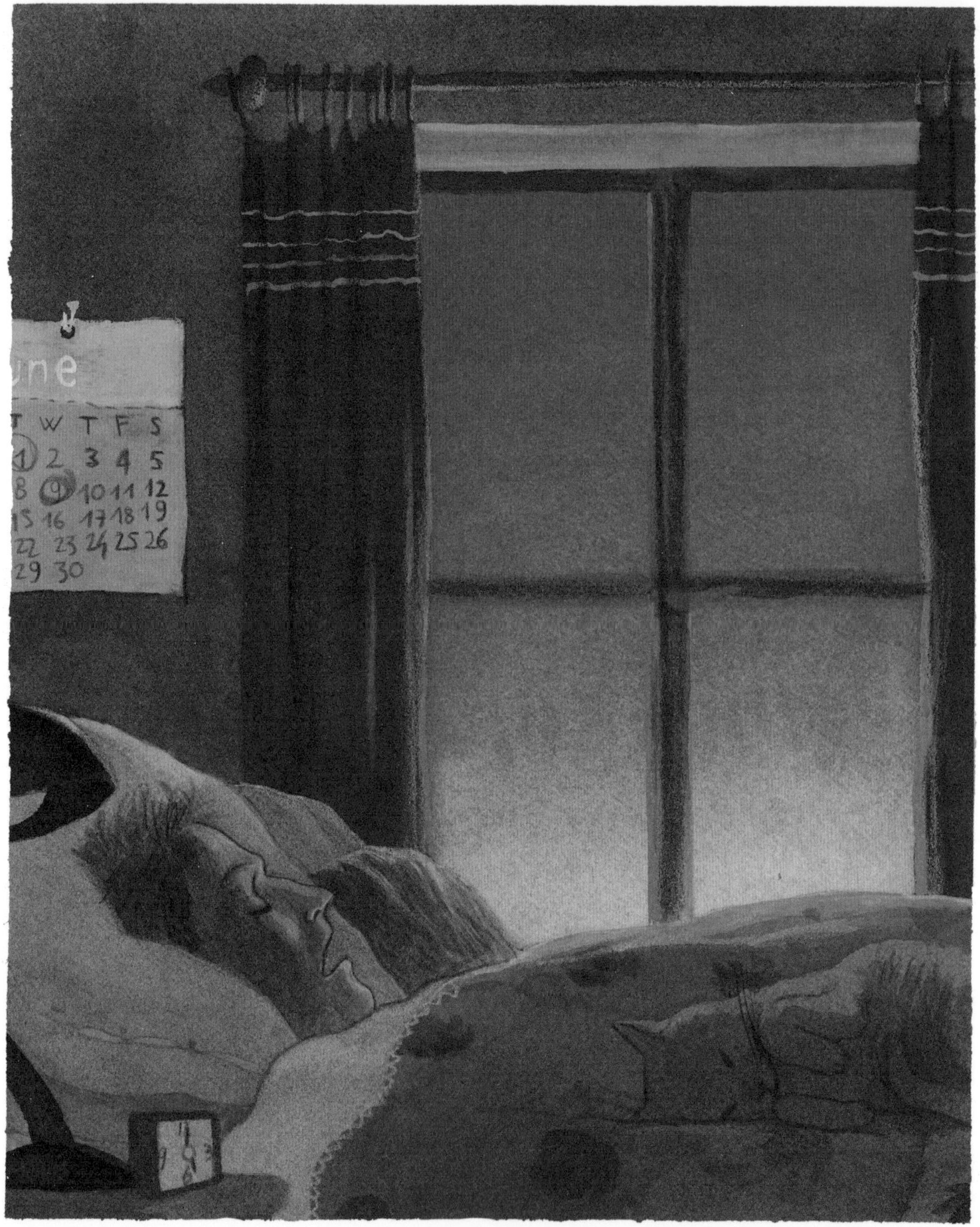
une
T W T F S
1 2 3 4 5
8 9 10 11 12
15 16 17 18 19
22 23 24 25 26
29 30

CYCLONE
PHENOMENES

AUTORAMA

10

ADING

TICKETS
CLOSED
♫
PALM READING
LA LUNE
♪
TIN
. . .

CASH

TIN
CAN